The Three Goats

DEAR CAREGIVER, The *Beginning-to-Read* series is a carefully written collection of classic readers you may remember from your own childhood. Each book features text comprised of common sight words to provide your child ample practice reading the words that appear most frequently in written text. The many additional details in the pictures enhance the story and offer the opportunity for you to help your child expand oral language and develop comprehension.

Begin by reading the story to your child, followed by letting him or her read familiar words and soon your child will be able to read the story independently. At each step of the way, be sure to praise your reader's efforts to build his or her confidence as an independent reader. Discuss the pictures and encourage your child to make connections between the story and his or her own life. At the end of the story, you will find reading activities and a word list that will help your child practice and strengthen beginning reading skills.

Above all, the most important part of the reading experience is to have fun and enjoy it!

Shannon Cannon

Shannon Cannon,
Literacy Consultant

Norwood House Press • P.O. Box 316598 • Chicago, Illinois 60631
For more information about Norwood House Press please visit our website at
www.norwoodhousepress.com or call 866-565-2900.

LIBRARY OF CONGRESS CATALOGING-IN-PUBLICATION DATA

Hillert, Margaret.
   The three goats / by Margaret Hillert ; illustrated by Mel Pekarsky.— Rev. and expanded
library ed.
      p. cm. — (Beginning to read series. Fairy tales and folklore)
   Summary: Simple retelling of the traditional tale about three billy goats who trick a troll
that lives under the bridge. Includes related activities.
   ISBN-13: 978-1-59953-027-7 (library edition : alk. paper)
   ISBN-10: 1-59953-027-9 (library edition : alk. paper) [1. Fairy tales. 2. Folklore—
Norway. 3. Readers.] I. Pekarsky, Mel, ill. II. Asbjxrnsen, Peter Christen, 1812-1885. Tre
bukkene Bruse. English. III. Title. IV. Series.
   PZ8.H5425Th 2006
   398.2—dc22   2005033495

The Three Goats

by Margaret Hillert

Illustrated by Mel Pekarsky

NORWOOD HOUSE PRESS

5

See the goats.
One, two, three goats.
Goats can run and jump.

The little goat said, "I want something.
I want to find something.
Away I go."

See the goat go.
The little goat can go up.
Up, up, up.

Look down here.

Here is something funny.

Run, run, run.
Jump, jump, jump.
Here I go.

Little goat, you can not go.
I want you, little goat.
Here I come.

Not I, not I.
Oh, help, help.
Away I go.
Jump, jump, jump.

Oh my, oh my.
See the little goat run away.

Here I come.
I want something.
I can come up here.

Goat, goat.
Come down.
Come down to me.
I want you.

Not I, not I.
I can run away.
Run, run, run.
And jump, jump, jump.

Oh my, oh my.
The goat can run and jump.
The goat can run away.

Big goat wants something.
See the big, big goat.

Here I come.
Here I come.

I see you, big goat.
I want you.
Come down here.

Not I.
You can not make me come down.
Come up here to me.

Look, big goat, look.
Here I come for you.

And—
Here you go!
Down.
Down.
Down.

See here.
See here.
We can run.

We can jump.
We can play.
We can run and play.

READING REINFORCEMENT

The following activities support the findings of the National Reading Panel that determined the most effective components for reading instruction are: Phonemic Awareness, Phonics, Vocabulary, Fluency, and Text Comprehension.

Phonemic Awareness: The /j/ sound

Substitution: Say the words on the left to your child. Ask your child to repeat the word, changing the first sound to /j/.

bump = jump	point = joint	far = jar	mug = jug
hog = jog	pet = jet	wig = jig	pail = jail

Phonics: The letter J j

1. Demonstrate how to form the letters **J** and **j** for your child.

2. Have your child practice writing **J** and **j** at least three times each.

3. Ask your child to point to the word in the book that starts with the letter **j**.

4. Write down the following words and ask your child to circle the letter **j** in each word:

jam	jet	Japan	joy	jump	jungle
jar	jingle	jog	jeep	jelly	June

Vocabulary: Personal Pronouns

1. Explain to your child that words that can be substituted for the names of people are called pronouns.

2. Write the following words on separate pieces of paper:

I	me	he	she	we	they

3. Read each word to your child and ask your child to repeat it.

4. Mix the words up. Point to a word and ask your child to read it. Provide clues if your child needs them.

5. Read the following sentences to your child. Ask your child to provide an appropriate pronoun to complete the sentence.

   • The three goats in the story wanted to cross the bridge. _____ all liked to run and jump.

   • Our classroom is a busy place. _____ read books, sing songs, and help each other.

   • Our teacher, Mr. Jones is very nice. _____ helps us learn how to read and count.

   • Reading is fun for me. ____ like to read fairy tale stories.

   • Miss Smith is our principal. Every morning ____ greets us when we come to school.

   • Yesterday was my birthday. My friends sang a song for _____.

Fluency: Shared Reading

1. Reread the story to your child at least two more times while your child tracks the print by running a finger under the words as they are read. Ask your child to read the words he or she knows with you.

2. Reread the story taking turns, alternating readers between sentences or pages.

Text Comprehension: Discussion Time

1. Ask your child to retell the sequence of events in the story.

2. To check comprehension, ask your child the following questions:

   • Where were the goats trying to go in the story?

   • Why did the troll want the goats? How do you know?

   • How did the big goat help?

WORD LIST

The Three Goats uses the 36 words listed below.

This list can be used to practice reading the words that appear in the text. You may wish to write the words on index cards and use them to help your child build automatic word recognition. Regular practice with these words will enhance your child's fluency in reading connected text.

and	go	make	said
away	goat (s)	me	see
		my	something
big	help		
	here	not	the
can			three
come	I	oh	to
	is	one	two
down			
	jump	play	up
find			
for	little	run	want
funny	look		
			you

Photograph by Glenna Washburn

ABOUT THE AUTHOR Margaret Hillert has written over 80 books for children who are just learning to read. Her books have been translated into many different languages and over a million children throughout the world have read her books. She first started writing poetry as a child and has continued to write for children and adults throughout her life. A first grade teacher for 34 years, Margaret is now retired from teaching and lives in Michigan where she likes to write, take walks in the morning, and care for her three cats.

ABOUT THE ADVISER Shannon Cannon contributed the activities pages that appear in this book. Shannon serves as a literacy consultant and provides staff development to help improve reading instruction. She is a frequent presenter at educational conferences and workshops. Prior to this she worked as an elementary school teacher and as president of a curriculum publishing company.